JP

WHAT SHOULD A HIPPO WEAR?

by Jane Sutton

Illustrated by Lynn Munsinger

OLD CHARLES TOWN LIBRARY
2 0 E. WA HINGTON ST.
CHARLES TOWN, W VA. 25 114

Houghton Mifflin Company·Boston·1979

83006447

To Al
for a thousand reasons

Library of Congress Cataloging in Publication Data

Sutton, Jane.
  What should a Hippo wear?

  SUMMARY: For the jungle dance, Bertha, a hippopotamus,
invents an eyecatching outfit only to discover that her
date, Fred, invited her for her plain old everyday self.
  [1. Hippopotamus–Fiction.   2. Jungle stories]
I. Munsinger, Lynn.   II. Title.
PZ7.S96824Wh   [E]   78-24005

COPYRIGHT © 1979 BY JANE SUTTON

COPYRIGHT © 1979 BY LYNN MUNSINGER

ALL RIGHTS RESERVED. NO PART OF THIS WORK MAY BE

REPRODUCED OR TRANSMITTED IN ANY FORM BY ANY MEANS,

ELECTRONIC OR MECHANICAL, INCLUDING PHOTOCOPYING AND

RECORDING, OR BY ANY INFORMATION STORAGE OR RETRIEVAL

SYSTEM, WITHOUT PERMISSION IN WRITING FROM THE PUBLISHER.

PRINTED IN THE UNITED STATES OF AMERICA

P 10 9 8 7 6 5 4 3 2 1

Bertha was lying in the cool mud when the telephone rang.

"Wouldn't you know it?" she thought. "The phone always rings right in the middle of my mud bath."

Bertha got out of the mud and went to the telephone. "It's probably a wrong number," she thought. But she hoped that it wasn't.

"Hello," said Bertha.

"Hello," said the soft voice on the other end of the telephone. "It's Fred . . . I was wondering," he said shyly. "The jungle dance is tonight and . . ."

"Yes?" said Bertha.

"Would you like to go to the jungle dance with me?" Fred asked.

"My goodness," said Bertha. "I would love to go."

"Good," said Fred. "I will pick you up when the sun goes down."

Bertha hung up the phone. She paced around her mud hole and thought about the dance. She hoped that Fred knew how to dance cheek to cheek. And she hoped that she wouldn't step on his feet.

But what could she wear? She only owned one dress and she had gotten so big that it didn't fit anymore. There was no time to go on a diet now.

Just then, a parrot flew overhead, holding a banner in his beak. The banner said: "Shop at the Jungle Dress Shop. We specialize in large sizes."

"That's for me!" snorted Bertha. She grabbed her pocketbook and hurried to the dress shop.

"May I help you?" asked the sales lady.

"Yes," said Bertha. "I need a dress to wear to the jungle dance."

"I have just the thing," said the sales lady. "It's the latest style."

"Ooh! It's beautiful," Bertha said.

She stretched and tugged and wriggled the dress over her head.
When she had it on, she looked at herself in the mirror.

"My my!" said Bertha. "I don't look half bad, if I do say so
myself!"

Bertha was so pleased with the dress that she started dancing in front of the mirror. But when she wiggled her hips and kicked her legs in the air, the dress split at the seams.

"Oh no!" cried Bertha. She took off the dress and gave it to the sales lady. "This dress only fits when I stand still," she said. "Do you have another dress I could try on?"

"I'm sorry, we don't," said the sales lady. "That was the biggest dress we had."

"It was such a pretty dress . . . while it lasted," Bertha said. She stomped out the door.

"Now what can I do?" Bertha wondered as she walked through the jungle.

"Ouch!" said a rock underneath Bertha's foot.

Bertha looked down and saw that it wasn't a rock at all. She had stepped on Florence.

"Excuse me," said Bertha. "I was thinking so hard that I didn't notice you."

"That's all right," said Florence. "Lots of animals mistake me for a rock lately. What were you thinking about?"

"I have nothing to wear to the jungle dance," said Bertha. "I can't find a dress big enough to fit me."

"What you need is a handmade dress," said Florence. "I can make you a dress that will fit you just fine."

"Oh, will you?" asked Bertha.

"Certainly," said Florence. "Now stop looking so sad and let me take your measurements."

First, Florence measured Bertha's neck. "Forty-six inches," she said. Then she measured how long Bertha was from her head to her tail and said, "Six and a half feet."

It took Florence almost an hour to measure Bertha. When she finished, Bertha asked, "What time will my dress be ready?"

"Well," said Florence, "I'll have to buy cloth and thread, cut out a pattern, sew . . . I think I can finish your dress in about two and a half weeks."

"But the dance is tonight!" said Bertha.

"Why didn't you say so in the first place?" asked Florence. "A handmade dress takes time!"

Bertha was so disappointed that she just walked away.

Soon she saw Ralph lying in front of Ralph's Arts and Crafts Store.

"Hello, Bertha," Ralph said. "You look so unhappy! Maybe something from my store will make you feel better."

"Thank you," said Bertha, "but I don't need any arts and crafts supplies. I need a dress to wear to the jungle dance."

Ralph stood up and straightened his mane. "I have something that you can use to make just the dress you want in about ten minutes," he said. He handed her a box of paints. "Use your imagination! Paint yourself a dress!" he said.

"That's a fine idea," said Bertha as she took the paints.

"Stop by again," Ralph roared. "We have something for everyone at Ralph's Arts and Crafts Store!"

Bertha ran back to her mud hole. She looked at the pretty colors in the paint box. Then she picked up the paint brush and started to paint. By the time she was finished, she was covered with polka dots from head to tail.

"This is quite an original dress!" thought Bertha. "And it fits me perfectly. But I need some shoes to go with it."

Bertha went to borrow shoes from her neighbors, Polly and Molly. She knocked on their tree trunk.

"Who's there?" shouted Polly.

"It's your neighbor," said Bertha. "I came to borrow a pair of shoes to wear to the jungle dance."

"Bertha! We hardly recognized you," said Molly.

"We never saw a polka dot hippo before," said Polly. "Wait a minute and we'll see what we can find."

Bertha heard them moving around in the branches, searching for the shoes.

Soon Polly and Molly climbed down from the tree. "I'm afraid we can't find two shoes of the same color," said Molly.

Bertha put on the shoes. They were so tight that they made her feet hurt, but she didn't care. "These shoes look wonderful with my new dress!" said Bertha. "Thank you so much."

Bertha stumbled back to her mud hole. "I hope these shoes don't make me stumble at the dance," thought Bertha. "Everyone will think I'm clumsy."

Back at the mud hole, Bertha still felt something was missing from her outfit. "I need some make-up," she decided.

Bertha used the rest of the paints to color her eyelids.

Then she pasted pieces of grass on her eyelashes with mud.

"What lovely long eyelashes!" she thought.

Then she crushed some bright red berries on her mouth to make lipstick.

Finally, she smeared reddish mud on her cheeks to make them rosy.

"Now, I am ready for the dance," she thought. "Wait until Fred sees how beautiful I look! Here he comes now."

When Fred got to Bertha's mud hole, he stopped and stared at her. "Excuse me, miss," he said. "Do you know where Bertha is?"

"*I* am Bertha," she said. She fluttered her long eyelashes at him.

"There must be some mistake," said Fred. "I'm looking for the Bertha I invited to the jungle dance. She doesn't wear make-up or fancy clothes."

"But everyone tries to look nice when they go to a dance!" snorted Bertha.

"I guess so," said Fred. "But the Bertha I asked to the dance doesn't have to dress up to look nice. She looks fine just the way she is. Have you seen her anywhere?"

Bertha didn't know what to say. She wished she hadn't put on fancy clothes and make-up. The shoes only made her feet hurt and the make-up only made her face sticky. Then she had an idea.

"Wait right here," she said to Fred. "I will find the Bertha you invited to the dance."

Bertha ran to the river. She pulled off the grass eyelashes. She
kicked off the shoes. She jumped in the river and washed off the
painted dress and the make-up.

Then she hurried back to the mud hole, happy to be feeling like herself again.

"Hello, Fred," she said.

"Hello, Bertha," he said. "My, you look nice!"

"Thank you," said Bertha happily.

"There was another Bertha here a minute ago," said Fred. "Where is she now?"

"Oh . . . um . . . she went for a swim in the river," said Bertha.

"Listen!" said Fred. "The dance music is starting. Let's go!"

And off they went.

The jungle dance was wonderful. Bertha and Fred said hello to
all their friends.

Then Fred bent his long neck down to Bertha and they danced cheek to cheek. Bertha didn't step on his feet once. In fact, she was very graceful.

JP   83006447
Sutton, Jane
What should a hippo wear?

OLD CHARLES TOWN LIBRARY

CHARLES TOWN, W. VA 25414